CLARE'S happiest when COOKING,
With bowl and wooden spoon.
She loves to bake a currant cake —
It's gobbled up too soon!

DOLORES is a DOGGY sort,
So many pups she's got
That when she takes them on a walk,
They tie her in a knot!

ELIZABETH likes EATING,
It is her favourite game!
If she won't stop, then she'll go pop,
And that would be a shame.

GILL'S hobby is star-GAZING,
And through her telescope
She's trying to count up every star —
I think she's got a hope.

FENELLA'S into FISHING,
She loves to net a newt.
The other day, I'm sad to say,
She only caught a boot!

LOUISE keeps writing LETTERS,
She's got a pen-pal, too,
And when the postman comes, he calls,
"Another one for you!"

MEG means to be a MODEL,
And move with charm and grace.
In front of Mummy's looking-glass,
She's making-up her face.

Turn to the back of the book.

£3.45

Printed and published by D. C. Thomson & Co., Ltd.,
Dundee and London.

Dear Girls,
Here is another great **Twinkle Book** specially for you. **Santa's secret helper, The Christmas moon, Melanie's magic day** and **Miss Mimosa Brown** are just some of the super stories you will find inside.

You'll also enjoy reading about your favourite "**Twinkle**" friends— **Nurse Nancy, Sam, My Baby Brother** and **Silly Milly.**

There are lots of interesting puzzles to do, too— and an exciting game to play!

Love from,

Twinkle

This book belongs to :—

Name _Sally Joy Boyle_

Address _18 Bawthorp Rd wisbech_

_____

_____

Nurse Nancy

1 — It was almost Christmas, and Nurse Nancy, who worked at the Dollies Hospital, decided to decorate the ward. She soon found a box full of tinsel and baubles.

2 — The toy patients were looking a little sad, and Nancy hoped that the decorations would cheer them up. Soon the nurse was hard at work.

3 — But even when she'd finished, the toys *still* looked glum. "I don't think they're going to enjoy Christmas much," Nancy sighed.

4 — Later, Nancy went to visit her friend, Jill, who was in hospital for a few days. Nancy thought how nice the ward looked with its decorations. Jill *was* pleased to see her chum.

5 — Jill told Nancy that she would be in hospital over Christmas. "But I'm looking forward to it," she smiled. "We play games, and open presents, and Santa visits us, too."

6 — This gave Nancy an idea, and she had a quiet word with the nurse who worked on the ward. The nurse happily agreed to Nancy's plan.

7 — So, on Christmas Day, Nancy and Colin, the ambulance driver, carefully carried the patients into the hospital ambulance. The toys *were* puzzled.

8 — When everyone was ready, Nancy told Colin to take the toys to the local hospital. This confused the toys even more! Can *you* guess why they were going there?

You can colour this picture using your paints or crayons.

9 — Nancy had decided to take the toys to the hospital, to join in with the fun. Soon, everyone was having a super time. "The toys aren't sad now," smiled Colin.

10 — "I'm *so* glad we came," Nancy chuckled in agreement. "I knew this would be a happy place to be on Christmas Day." And the toys thought so, too!

Santa's secret helper

1 — It was almost Christmas, and little Pauline Smart was busy wrapping some presents when she got a lovely surprise. "Hoorah!" she cried. "It's snowing!"

2 — Pauline hurried outside to build a snowman, and when she'd finished, she *was* pleased. "He looks real," she grinned, and *he* seemed to smile back!

3 — That evening, Pauline decided to write her letter to Santa. "Put it under the tree," suggested Mummy. "Then Santa will be able to collect it." "That's a good idea," Pauline replied, chuckling.

4 — But next morning, Pauline's letter from Santa was *still* there. "Perhaps he was too busy," she sighed, and hurried off to school.

5 — But when Pauline arrived, she discovered that Santa hadn't collected any of her friends' letters either! "And I put mine out *days* ago," wailed Laura Craig.

6 — That evening, Pauline went outside to see if she could spot Santa. "Oh, where *are* you?" she cried. "Would you like to go and find him?" a voice asked.

7 — To Pauline's amazement, it was the *snowman* who had spoken! "I — I would like to," she stammered. "Well, come with me," smiled her friend.

8 — In one magical moment, Pauline found herself soaring up into the night sky. "To Santaland!" cried the snowman.

More to follow . . .

Ted and Zed

from Outer Space

TED and Zed, the space bear and dog, wondered why their friends were so miserable. "We hoped it would snow," sighed Sarah. "What's snow?" asked Zed.

2 — "You don't know what *snow* is?" gasped the girls, and they tried to explain. "There's some on the mountains," Sally cried. "Then let's go," said Ted, and they all climbed into Ted's flying car.

3 — Ted and Zed *loved* the snow when they landed on a mountain. "Snow is super!" called Zed, jumping about and kicking it everywhere. "It's *great*," grinned Ted, collecting a huge ball of snow. "Let's take *loads* back with us."

4 — Before the snow could melt, they zoomed to the spaceship. Back home, Ted brought out a weird machine and put the giant snowball inside it.

5 — "What are you doing, Ted?" asked the girls. Just then, the machine spurted out more snow.

6 — Soon, children came from *everywhere* to play in the special snow made by Ted and Zed.

A rainy day

What shall I play with now because
　　It's raining and I'm staying in?
I *could* dress my new doll or wind
　　My clockwork clown, who makes me grin.

My sewing box needs tidying,
　　The pins and cottons put in right.
And there's my teddy's scarf to knit
　　In golden yellow, green and white.

Perhaps I'll do some cutting out,
　　From comics Grandad bought for me.
Then paste all kinds of pictures in
　　To make a special scrapbook, see.

I *could* dust my doll's house and then
　　Clean all the windows till they shine.
Next brush the carpets, polish floors
　　And wash the velvet curtains fine.

Why, there's a *rainbow* in the sky!
　　From red to violet run its shades.
Now *that's* what I'll do — get my paints
　　And paint it fast before it fades!

The Christmas moon

THERE was great activity in the Rabbit household as Mummy Rabbit began to make the Christmas pudding.

"Can we help?" cried the children.

"Roddy can fetch the flour and Robert can fetch the fruit," Mummy said.

"What can *I* do?" asked Baby Fluff.

"You can bring the spoons," answered Mummy, smiling.

"Don't forget to wish," laughed Daddy when Mummy began to stir the mixture.

"I'm wishing for a train," Robert said.

"I'm wishing for a car," Roddy shouted.

"What about you, Fluff?" asked Mummy.

"I would like the moon," Fluff whispered shyly.

"The *moon*?" scoffed Robert.

"I don't want to keep it," whispered Fluff. "I only want to hold it."

Fluff had never seen anything as beautiful as the moon.

"If only I could hold it just for a moment," she thought, but the moon was *so* far away.

Later, downstairs, Mr and Mrs Rabbit were busy hanging decorations.

"Well, well. Look what I've found," exclaimed Daddy, holding up a white balloon. "I'll hang it from the ceiling."

Upstairs, Fluff tossed and turned restlessly as the wind rattled her window. Suddenly, a loud gust of wind woke her.

At first she couldn't understand why it was so dark, then she looked out of the window and gasped.

The moon was no longer in the sky. Fluff jumped out of bed and ran down the stairs.

"The moon has gone!" she cried. "Someone has stolen the moon!"

Fluff lifted a tearful face — then saw the white balloon hanging from the ceiling!

"The moon!" she cried, pointing to the balloon. "You've got me the moon for Christmas!"

Fluff had never seen a balloon before and she really did think it was the moon! Daddy placed the balloon in Fluff's arms.

"What are you going to do with the moon now, Fluff?" asked her mummy.

Fluff looked thoughtfully through the window. The sky was so dark. It was *much* nicer when the moon shone down.

"I'm going to put it back in the sky," she said at last.

Outside, Fluff let the balloon go and it sailed out of sight.

Fluff sighed, then a wonderful thing happened. The moon peeped out from behind the clouds.

"There it is!" Fluff cried. "It's back in the sky!"

The moon shone down as Fluff closed her eyes, back in bed.

"Won't Robert and Roddy be surprised when I tell them I've held the moon in my arms?" she thought sleepily.

Picture puzzles

Can you find six differences between the two pictures of the Snow Queen?

Which two treasure chests are exactly the same?

Join the dots on the right to find the Snow Queen's helper, then lead them both through the maze to the royal coach

Sam

SHONA MACGREGOR has a clever sheepdog called Sam. They live on a farm in the Scottish Highlands.

Shona had invited her best friend, Lucinda, to stay for the weekend. When they went outside, they had to put on warm clothes, for the weather was bitterly cold.

"There's heavy snow coming," said Shona's dad, anxiously looking at the overcast sky. "We must get the sheep and cattle on to lower ground."

So, all that morning, Sam worked hard and by lunchtime, he'd rounded up nearly all the animals.

"Well done, Sam," cried Lucinda. "You're as clever as Shona says."

"He's cleverer than that," laughed Mr MacGregor. "Sometimes he tells *me* what to do."

"Well, I hope he tells us to get indoors and have something to eat," joked Shona. "I'm *starving*!"

Soon it was snowing heavily and Sam became restless. He scratched and whined at the door to go out.

"He's worried because Cherrycup is still on the hill," said Dad. "We couldn't find her and she's due to calf soon."

2 — Shona had a suggestion, however.

"If it keeps snowing like this," she said, "there will soon be enough lying for Lucinda and me to go sledging. We can take Sam with us and perhaps *we'll* find Cherrycup."

Mr MacGregor thought that was a good idea, so that afternoon the girls set off with Shona's toboggan.

4 — "Clever Sam," cried Shona, hugging the sheepdog. "You remembered that Cherrycup calved here before."

Sam nosed the calf and gave a little whimper.

"The calf is freezing," exclaimed Shona. "We must get him home quickly."

The calf couldn't walk in the deep snow, so Shona lifted him on to the toboggan and she and Lucinda began to pull him along behind her.

Suddenly, Lucinda stumbled over the tip of a snow-covered rock.

"My ankle!" she cried painfully. "I've twisted it. I don't think I'll be able to walk!"

"Don't worry," said Shona, helping her friend. "I'll pull *you* home, too."

However, no matter how hard Shona tugged, she couldn't shift the heavy toboggan.

"It's getting dark," she sighed. "What can we do?"

Sam knew. He lifted the toboggan rope with his teeth.

"Sam's telling us we can harness him to the toboggan and he'll help pull it!" cried Lucinda.

3 — As they moved on to higher ground, Sam barked then bounded towards an overhanging rock. There, sheltering, were Cherrycup and her newly-born calf!

5 — At the farmhouse, Shona's dad was setting out to look for the girls when Sam loomed out of the thick-falling snow, with everyone right behind.

"I might have known Sam would see everyone home safely," Dad chuckled.

Over hot cocoa, Shona told Dad what had happened, while Mum bandaged Lucinda's foot.

"It's only a sprain," she reassured the little girl.

On television, a programme about Husky dogs had just begun.

"Sam is better than any Husky!" cried Lucinda.

Sam barked in agreement — and outside a cow mooed.

"Even Cherrycup agrees with that," laughed Shona. *"She's thanking Sam for his help, too!"*

Melanie's magic day

1 — Mervin the magician was old and *very* forgetful. One day, Queen Gladys arrived with Princess Melanie and ordered him to make a growing potion.

2 —"She needs to gain an extra inch or two," shrieked the Queen. Mervin set to work. The only trouble was he couldn't quite remember what to put in it.

3 — When the potion was ready, the little princess *gulped* it down. It certainly made her grow, but by feet instead of inches! She was soon too big for Mervin's room.

4 — Poor Mervin couldn't remember how to change the princess back. Melanie, meanwhile, was having a wonderful time. She ate things she shouldn't . . .

5 — ... and was *so* big, her governess couldn't keep her within the castle walls — she just stepped over them! Mervin tried his hardest, but it was no use.

6 — One day, Mervin's apprentices had an idea. "Perhaps if you take some of your own memory potion," they explained, "it might help you to remember."

7 — Mervin swallowed the potion, and within seconds remembered the very spell. Melanie wasn't very pleased, she *had* enjoyed being big, but Queen Gladys was overjoyed.

8 — From that day on, every morning, along with his porridge, Mervin took a spoonful of memory potion, and never forgot anything again.

Baby Brother's year

IN JANUARY, when the snow
Lies thick on frozen ground,
Ben makes a snowman tall and proud —
The best for miles around.

IN FEBRUARY, Ben runs to pick
The catkins, soft and yellow.
"The lambs have tails like catkins, too!"
Exclaims the funny fellow.

THE wind blows merrily in MARCH.
The sun is shining bright.
"Let's *march* up to the hill!" laughs Ben.
"It's time to fly my kite."

ONE APRIL day, I thought I heard
A cuckoo singing bright.
But it was just that cheeky Ben,
Whistling with all his might!

THE bluebells come in MAY. For Mum,
  A great, big bunch we bring.
"Oh, aren't they beautiful!" she cries.
  Ben grins, "I wish they'd *ring* !"

IN JUNE, we go out picnicking,
  With strawberries for tea.
Somehow, the rascal always gets
  The biggest one, you see!

JULY'S the month for holidays,
  Off to the sea we go.
"Just watch me have a swim!" cries Ben,
  And puts in one wee toe.

IN AUGUST, it is harvest time,
  There's plenty to be done.
But like Boy Blue, Ben falls asleep,
  And snoozes in the sun.

SEPTEMBER, and the apples grow
   Along the bough, so red.
Ben tries to shake one down, but oh!
   It lands upon his head!

OCTOBER — days of falling leaves.
   Ben sweeps them in a pile.
But *whoosh* the wind blows them away . . .
   (Oh dear, I have to smile!)

FIFTH of NOVEMBER — fireworks time!
   Bright stars of red and blue.
Ben likes the *bangers* best of all.
   (Though hot dogs are good, too!)

DECEMBER — Christmas comes around,
   With goodies on the tree.
"A happy Christmas to you, sis!"
   Says little Ben to me.

Twin tricks

TESS sighed as her twin brother, Tom, got ready for his football match.

"Can't I play too?" she asked.

"No way," came the reply. "We don't want *girls* playing in *our* team!"

"Oh well," thought Tess. "They can't stop me *watching*."

As she looked on, Tess thought to herself how *she* was just as good at playing as the boys. If only they'd give her a chance!

Back home, Tess practised football on her own, but what she *really* wanted, was a *proper* game of football!

Just then, a friend came to call.

"Oh, hi, Stacey," Tess smiled. "Fancy a game of football?"

Stacey smiled and wrinkled her nose.

"Not really — but Jill and I are going to play with my skipping rope. Coming?"

Tess sighed and nodded her head — it was better than doing nothing.

A few days later, Tom came back from his latest football match, bursting with excitement.

"You'll never guess," he gasped. "We're through to the finals of the Football Championships! Isn't that great?"

Tess smiled in agreement — Tom was *so* lucky!

But, on the day of the final, Tom wasn't very lucky at all!

"Oh, Tess," he croaked from his sick bed, "I can't play like this! I feel awful."

Tess sat down on her brother's bed and handed him another tissue.

"Can I do anything to help?" she asked. "Do you want me to phone someone and tell them you won't be there?"

Tom glanced at his alarm clock and shook his head. "No one will be home now — they'll be on their way to the park. You'll have to go round there to tell them."

Quickly, Tess grabbed her coat and dashed from the house. Luckily, the match was being played at the park just along the road.

She spotted Tom's friends gathered beside the changing hut, but before she had a chance to speak, she overheard their conversation.

"Let's hope Tom doesn't call off — with Craig and John both down with flu, we really need him."

"Yeah — we'll only have ten men without him."

Tess stopped in her tracks. She couldn't tell them about Tom now — but what could she do? Turning quickly, she hurried back home. She had a plan!

Tom's football kit lay ready in the hall. Tess snatched it up, then quietly tiptoed into her room to change into the football strip. Next, she tucked her long hair into a cap.

Looking at herself in a mirror, she gave a smile — they'd never know the difference! She looked *just* like Tom!

When Tess arrived back at the park, the game was just about to start, so she hurried on to the pitch and took up Tom's usual position.

"Whew! Thank goodness you've made it!" grinned Graham, one of the team. "Hope you're on form today!"

But Tess could only smile a reply — for the game had begun!

Tess couldn't remember when she'd had so much fun — all her practising against the garage door was put to good use as she ran up and down the pitch, kicking and passing the ball.

"You're playing great today, Tom," shouted the manager from the sidelines. "Keep it up!"

Tess smiled happily — she always knew she could play!

All too soon, the game was over — and to Tess's delight, 'her' team won!

"It's all thanks to you, Tom!" someone said. "Three cheers for Tom!"

"But I'm *not* Tom," Tess told the amazed team. "Look!"

With that, she pulled off her cap, letting her hair fall about her shoulders.

"Tess! You!" gasped Graham. "I don't believe it!"

"*Now* will you let me play?" she pleaded. "Please!"

A cheer went up, and Tess found herself being carried shoulder-high towards her home. She knew she'd never have to play football on her own again!

Winter fun·time

You can colour this picture using your paints or crayons.

Which two skaters are the same?

Lead Sammy Squirrel through the maze to the ice hockey puck.

Rearrange the first letters of each object, round the letter "n", to find a super winter pastime.

Ans. Sledging.

Can you find six differences between these two pictures?

Polly

Merry Christma

Happy Christmas

1 — Polly Penguin lives in Snowland with her chums, Suki, Rodney and Peter. It was nearly Christmas, and Polly was searching for presents to give her friends.

2 — "Everything costs *so* much," she sighed. "I haven't nearly enough money to buy presents for everyone." Polly *did* feel sad as she gazed at all the expensive gifts.

ICES

MOULDING KIT

3 — Just then, Polly spotted Petra Polar Bear buying a large ice-cream. "I've just stocked up my freezer for Christmas," said Mrs Polar Bear. This gave Polly an idea.

4 — She hurried home and searched for her moulding kit. Then, filling a large jug with water, she set to work. "I'll make my chums *special* presents this year," she said.

5 — Christmas morning arrived, and Suki, Peter and Rodney arrived with Polly's presents. "Merry Christmas," they cheered. "Come inside," smiled Polly.

6 — Indoors, Polly opened the lid of her freezer. "Your presents are in here," she explained. The three chums *were* puzzled. What could Polly have got them?

7 — They soon found out when they pulled the wrapping from their gifts. Polly had made them special ice-gnomes for the garden!

8 — "These are super," laughed the chums. "And if we keep them outside, they'll never melt." Polly *was* glad, and they all gave a *Merry Christmas* cheer as they tucked into their mince pies!

Elfie

1 — Elfie secretly lives in Mary's doll's house. The little girl thinks there's *magic* at work when Elfie makes things happen! One day, they watched ice skating on TV.

2 — "Mummy, can *we* please go to the ice rink?" asked Mary, after the programme finished. Elfie was delighted when Mum agreed. "*I* love skating, too!" he cheered.

3 — When searching for her skates, Mary found an old mirror. "I'll clean it later and hang it in my room," she grinned. "Oh, do *hurry* up," cried Elfie impatiently.

4 — But at the ice rink, the elf was in for a disappointment. "I'm too *frightened* to join in," he wailed. "Those feet are too big and fast for a little chap like me."

5 — By the time he returned home, however, Elfie had an idea. He fetched Mary's old mirror, a tin of polish and two small rags, which he tied to his feet.

6 — After putting a little polish on the rags, Elfie jumped on to the mirror — and began to skate! "I'm having fun *and* polishing away the dirt," he cried happily.

7 — Very soon, the mirror was *so* shiny that Elfie could hardly keep his balance. "I'll have to stop now," he chuckled. "It's too slippery to skate on this any more!"

8 — Mary was *amazed* when she found the mirror. "It — it's been polished," she gasped. "It must be the magic." Elfie *did* laugh. "Not the magic," he grinned. "*Me*!"

Santa's secret helper

Part 2

9 — When Pauline and the snowman arrived in Santaland, she couldn't believe her eyes! "Is it always like this?" she asked. "It doesn't seem very well organised."

10 — Her friend explained that Santa had a bad cold. "And now there's no one to take charge," he sighed. "No wonder our letters weren't collected," said Pauline.

11 — The snowman took Pauline to visit Santa. "Is everything all right?" the old man asked. "Those silly elves can't do anything on their own." Pauline didn't want to worry Santa, so she told him all was well.

12 — The little girl decided to call a meeting of Santa's helpers, to tell them what she wanted them to do.

13 — Soon, everyone was busy. A group of elves set out to collect the letters sent to Santa, and Pauline made sure all the presents were wrapped up nicely.

14 — Not even the reindeer were forgotten about, as Pauline, and a few helpers, worked hard to make them look their best. "This *is* fun," the little girl smiled.

15 — They were all *so* busy, that they forgot all about the time. Then the town clock struck midnight. "It's Christmas Eve now," gasped an elf. "Only one day to go!"

16 — "And it's time for *you* to go home," the snowman told Pauline. "Oh, I *do* hope everything goes well!" The girl cried.

More to follow . . .

Ups and Downs

Four people can play this game. You will need a dice and a button counter for each player. Choose a column to start with, then take turns to throw the dice and move up the number of squares shown on the dice. If you land on a square with instructions, follow them. Once one column has been completed move on to the next and so on. The player who completes all four columns first wins.

Jessica's fancy dress

JESSICA was staying with her grandparents for a holiday. One day, as they were having their lunch, there was a knock at the door.

Jessica went with Grandpa to answer it and found Katie, the little girl from next door, standing there.

"Hello," smiled Katie. "I've come to see if Jessica would like to come to my party this afternoon."

"Oh thank you, I'd love that," replied Jessica. "Is it a *special* sort of party?"

"It's really a fancy dress party," explained Katie, "but if you haven't got a costume, it doesn't matter. Just come as you are."

"Super — I'll be there," Jessica assured her with a smile.

2 — When Katie went home, Jessica and Grandpa went back to their lunch.

"I wish I *did* have something to dress up in, though," sighed Jessica. "I didn't think to bring anything like *that* with me."

"Never mind," smiled Grandpa. "How would you like to help me in the garden until it's time for the party?"

"Oh, yes please," Jessica replied, and she hurried to finish her lunch.

"There's no need to rush," Granny told her. "Grandpa has to get changed into his gardening clothes first."

Grandpa went upstairs to put on his gardening clothes. When he came down, he was dressed in a torn jacket and had a battered old hat on his head.

"Oh, Grandpa," laughed Jessica. "You *do* look funny dressed like that."

"I know," her grandpa agreed, "but these old clothes are just right for gardening."

3 — Jessica put on her coat and wellies and she and Grandpa went out into the garden. Grandpa pointed to some tall plants.

"We need to tie up those plants," he explained. "Let's see if we can find any canes."

They looked in the garden shed and found some canes in a corner.

"What shall we use to tie the plants to the canes?" asked Jessica.

Grandpa laughed and took a ball made of different lengths of string out of his pocket.

"I never throw away string — it always comes in handy," he told her.

They had a busy time tying the plants to the canes. Jessica *did* enjoy helping Grandpa, even though it was messy work.

"That should make them grow up straight," said Grandpa when they'd finished. "Now, I think we've done enough for today. We'll go inside and have a cup of tea before it's time for your party."

4 — When they went back into the house, they found Granny making furry little mice.

"Oh, these are lovely," Jessica cried.

"I'm making them to sell at the village fete," Granny told her. "Now, let's see about tea, and afterwards you can change into your party dress."

Then, looking at Grandpa, she smiled, "I think *you'd* better get changed right now. You look just like an old scarecrow."

Grandpa looked thoughtful, then plonked his old hat on Jessica's head.

"Not bad," he chuckled. "Now see how my jacket fits."

"It's too big and the sleeves are much too long," Jessica protested, puzzled.

"That's where my string will come in handy again," said Grandpa. "I'll tie up the sleeves with string — and you can go to the party dressed as a *scarecrow.*"

Jessica thought it was a *super* idea.

"But what about trousers?" she asked.

"I could sew some bright patches to your play trousers," suggested Granny.

5 — While Granny stitched a red patch to one leg of Jessica's play trousers, and a spotty yellow patch to the other, Grandpa went to the garden shed and collected two short canes.

When he came back, he pushed them up the sleeves of his old jacket which Jessica was wearing. Then Granny tied Jessica's hair in two bunches with some more of Grandpa's string.

"Now, what shall I give you to take for a present?" asked Granny.

"One of your furry little mice would make a lovely present," suggested Grandpa. "And we'll tie another one to Jessica's hat. That will make her look even more like a scarecrow!"

Jessica had a *lovely* time at the party and had exciting news for Grandpa when he collected her.

"Katie loved her little mouse and *I* won a prize for my costume," she told him.

"I'm not surprised," laughed Grandpa. "You're the best scarecrow I've ever seen!"

Poppy's present

1 — It was Christmas Eve and Poppy realised she'd forgotten to buy her cousin, Hannah, a present.

2 — "The corner shop will still be open," Mummy told her. "If you hurry, you should be able to get something for Hannah there."

3 — On the way, Poppy spotted an old woman who had fallen.

4 — The old lady lived nearby, so Poppy offered to take her home. "I'll make you a nice cup of tea," she told her. The lady was very grateful.

5 — Poppy was glad to have helped, but when she saw the time, she realised that the shop would be shut. Now she wouldn't be able to buy a present.

6 — When the lady heard Poppy's problem, she took her to another room, filled with toys. "I make them for a toy shop," she explained. "Please take one."

7 — Poppy *was* pleased, and chose a pretty doll. She thanked the woman, and promised to visit another day. "Merry Christmas," Poppy smiled.

8 — Hannah thought the doll was lovely. Poppy smiled, too — for she'd made a new friend.

Patch

1 — Paula Perkins has a cute kitten called Patch. He likes to join in whatever Paula does. When her friend, Sarah, brought a puppy to visit, Patch was ready to have fun.

2 — Ember, the puppy, wanted to play, too — but not with Patch. *She* only wanted to play with Patch's toys. She collected them all into a pile and wouldn't let Patch have any.

3 — Paula and Sarah laughed, but Patch didn't think it funny. Every time the kitten tried to play with a toy, Ember snatched it away. The pup even chased Patch when he picked up a pom-pom!

4 — Later, Paula and Sarah brought out a basket of wool. "Now, now," scolded Sarah as Patch and Ember tried to play with the balls, "we don't want it tangled, do we?"

5 — But when Paula and Sarah left the room, the pets had a *super* time chasing the wool — and each other. They had found a game they could *both* play!

6 — What a mess the room was in when the girls returned — but Patch and Ember were fast asleep. That was something else they could do together!

Nancy's party time

NURSE NANCY is holding a special party for her friends. But will she be ready in time? Cut out or trace the counters on the opposite page — and use a dice to make your way round the board. The player to reach the finish first is the winner.

START

1

Nancy has forgotten the crackers! Miss a turn while she buys some. 2

3

4

5

6

Nancy can't find the fairy for the top of the tree. Go back one square to look for it. 7

8

9

10

Nancy offers her brother a treat if he helps wrap presents. Move on three squares. 11

12

13

14

15

16 Snow falls — and Nancy can't resist dashing out to build a snowman. Miss a turn.

17

24

25 Carol singers come visiting. Miss a turn while Nancy listens.

23

22 Phew — Nancy's tired! Stop for a break — and move back three squares.

26 A friend arrives early, and helps blow up balloons — move on one square.

21

20 Nancy mixes up fairy cakes in a flash. Move on one square.

27

28

19

29

18

30 It's party time! Merry Christmas!

FINISH

Make a Pop-up Puppet

To make your Ted pop-up puppet, cut a hole, big enough for a pencil to fit through, in the base of a yoghurt carton. Cut out the figures of Ted and Zed and stick Ted to a pencil. Next slip the pencil through the hole in the carton. Wind some tape round the pencil, below the carton, to stop it popping out too far. Now do the same to make Zed.

Ted

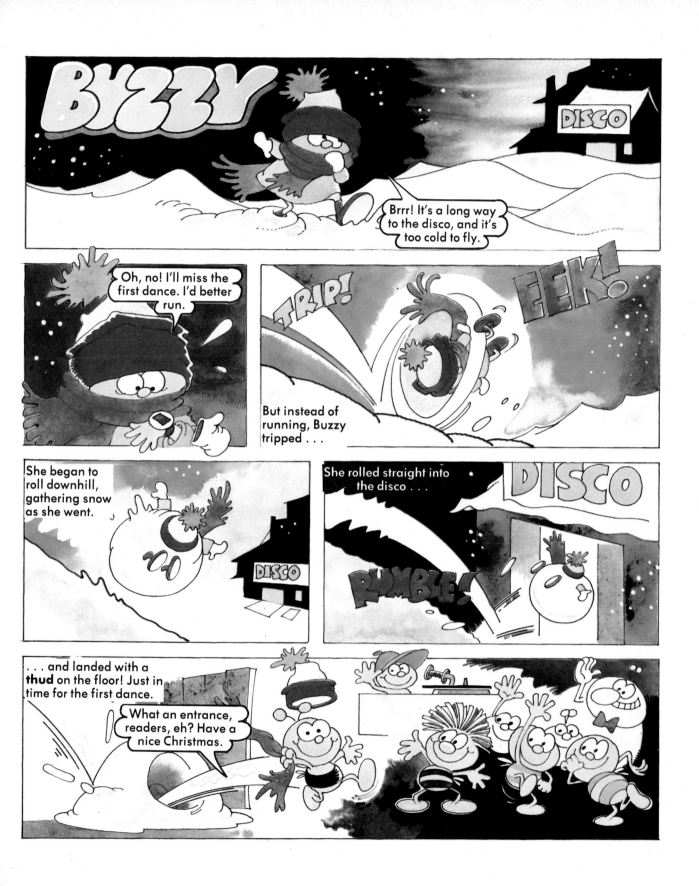

My favourite time

ALTHOUGH I like long summer days,
Sunbathing by the sea,
It's *Christmas* time I love the best,
With snow and pretty tree.

Now Christmas shopping is great fun,
There's lots of things to buy.
"Oh, what will I give everyone?"
You often hear me sigh!

Mum's mince pies are a Christmas treat
All piping hot with cream.
And Granny's special chocolate log,
It tastes just like a dream.

We love to build a snowman tall,
(If there is snow about!)
"Don't you think he looks like Dad?"
I hear my brother shout!

But Christmas day is best of all,
With presents, gifts and cheer.
And I'm so glad my favourite time
Comes every single year!

Home sweet home

SUGAR PLUM the fairy was fed up. She sat in her house made of sweets and sighed.

"Oh, I wish I didn't have to eat sweets all the time," she thought to herself.

You see, her walls were made of icing, her window frames were barley sugar, her furniture was made from liquorice . . . and her pillows were made of candy floss! Now, that might sound good to *you*, but Sugar Plum didn't *want* to eat sweets all day!

"But what can I do?" she asked her chum Peter Pixie. "I have to live *somewhere*, and it's so difficult to find a new house these days."

Peter nodded in agreement, and cut Sugar Plum another slice of mushroom pie.

"I wish *my* house was made of mushrooms, like yours," the fairy said wistfully as she tucked into her tea. "This pie is delicious."

But Peter didn't think so.

2 — "Mushrooms are so *boring,"* he complained. "I have them for breakfast, lunch and tea, and still they keep on growing. I just can't get rid of them!"

Sometimes living in Fairyland wasn't all fun!

After tea, Sugar Plum and Peter decided to go for a walk round their village.

Mr and Mrs Imp seemed quite happy in their gingerbread house, and Sugar Plum's cousin Flossy thought *her* loaf house was delicious!

"No one else seems to mind," sighed Peter. "It looks like we'll just have to get used to eating the same things all the time."

3 — Sugar Plum pointed to a colourful house just ahead of them.

"Look — Eddie the Elf's home's lovely, isn't it? All that fruit?"

Peter nodded in agreement. "Mmm . . . what could be nicer?"

The pair stopped to admire the tiny fruit trees that made up the elf's home.

As they stood, looking at the rosy apples, the plump plums and the juicy oranges, Eddie appeared carrying a large basket of fruit.

"Would you like some?" he asked them. "My house grows so much fruit, I can't use it all. It's just a nuisance!"

4 — Sugar Plum and Peter smiled sympathetically — they knew just how he felt!

And then, Peter had a rather splendid idea.

"Why don't we . . ." he cried, " . . . why don't we rebuild our houses using a bit from each other's? That way our houses will be made of lots of different things to eat, and we'd never get bored!"

Eddie and Sugar Plum jumped up and down with excitement! Why hadn't they thought of that before? The three chums danced with glee.

5 — Soon they were *very* busy — digging, planting and moving things about until they each had just the home they wanted!

Peter had mushroom furniture, chocolate walls, and a roof made from strawberry plants — Eddie kept fruit trees for *his* walls, but made his roof from a giant mushroom, and filled his rooms with sugar chairs and tables.

Sugar Plum decided to have *her* home made with apples, oranges and mushrooms but kept her candy floss pillows, because, she said, she just couldn't sleep on anything else!

6 — So Sugar Plum didn't have to have sweets for breakfast, lunch and tea, Peter had something else to eat apart from mushrooms, and Eddie's fruit trees didn't bother him any more!

Now the three chums had the nicest homes in Fairyland — and people travelled from all over just to see them. How everyone wished they had a home just like it!

"I am," thought tiny Sugar Plum, as she sat down to her tasty lunch of mushroom soup and fruit pie, "the luckiest fairy in Fairyland!"

And next time *you* go for a walk in the woods, or explore a park or garden — be careful of the mushrooms you pick, or the fruit trees you climb — it *could* be someone's home!

Father Christmas Fun

Which lead is pinned to Bobby's collar?

Can you find six differences between these two pictures?

Lead Santa through the maze to his sack of toys.

Join the dots to find this Christmas toy.

Rearrange the letters to see what this is.

STOCKING.

Which two reindeer are exactly the same?

1 — Silly Milly is always in trouble. Just before Christmas, Milly decided to shop for all her presents. "Hmm! Perhaps Mum would like some perfume," she thought.

2 — Milly spent the whole day in town, and eventually she found gifts for everyone. She was *so* organised, she even bought fancy paper and bows for each of them.

3 — That night, while Mum and Dad were busy in the kitchen, Milly wrapped the presents. There was ribbon and sticky tape everywhere except on the parcels!

4 — But, eventually Milly's Christmas gifts were wrapped and labelled — they *did* look nice. "I'm getting better," she grinned. "No accidents yet."

5 — Early on Christmas morning, Milly couldn't wait to hand out her presents. So, shouting for Mopsy, she rushed into Mum and Dad's room.

6 — "Oh, Milly," gasped Mum. "They look lovely." Milly beamed proudly. "Yes," she said. "And I didn't have a single mishap with them this year."

7 — But silly Milly had spoken too soon, for when everyone opened their gifts they *were* in for a surprise! Mum had a nice bone. Dad had pink slippers, and Mopsy had a pipe!

8 — "Ooops!" grinned Milly. "Well I suppose it wouldn't be the same without a muddle from me! Merry Christmas everyone!"

Santa's secret helper

Part 3

17 — The following morning, Pauline slept late. "My goodness," she thought. "I *am* tired." Then the little girl remembered all that had happened.

18 — Hurrying to the window, Pauline looked outside. "Oh, the snowman's back to normal," she sighed. "It must have all been a dream." Pauline *was* disappointed.

19 — That night, Pauline hung up her Christmas stocking. Suddenly, she heard a knocking sound at her bedroom window. "Who can that be?" she puzzled.

20 — It was the *snowman.* "Quickly!" he cried. "Santa needs your help to deliver your friends' presents. Those silly elves have mixed up all the labels!"

21 — Pauline hurried outside to help. He was right — the elves had jumbled up all the presents. "This one's for Laura," Pauline said. "She wanted a toy farm."

22 — "Thank goodness you're here," chuckled Santa. "If it weren't for you, all your chums would be opening the wrong presents in the morning."

23 — Next day, Pauline had her *own* presents to open. "You *have* got a lot!" Mummy cried. Pauline smiled — these presents were a 'thank you' from Santa.

24 — And Pauline, too, had a present for a special friend. "This is for *you,*" she whispered to the snowman. "For my best Christmas ever!"

THE END

Miss Mimosa Brown

BECCY'S mother was the first to see the cat as it peered through the garden gate.

"Beccy," Mrs Dean called softly, "come quickly. There's a brown cat at the gate."

Beccy left the jigsaw she was doing and tip-toed carefully down the path, calling, "Puss, puss, come and talk to me."

"Cats don't talk," said her mother. "They *purr*."

The brown cat wriggled through the ironwork gate and came to meet Beccy.

"I think *this* cat might be able to talk," said Beccy. "It's probably a brown witch's cat which fell off a broomstick."

Beccy's mum just laughed. "What an imagination you've got," she chuckled.

Beccy reached for the little silver tube hanging from the collar round their visitor's neck. Inside was a tiny piece of paper.

"Mimosa," Beccy read out. "Her name is Mimosa. I shall call her Miss Mimosa Brown!"

Mimosa gave a twitch of her fine, shiny whiskers, another twitch of her tail, then she offered Beccy her paw, before turning and walking into the house.

"She seems to like the idea of being Mimosa Brown," said Mrs Dean.

2 — Mimosa decided to explore her new surroundings. She stopped outside Beccy's bedroom.

"She *knows* it's my room," Beccy cried. "Wait a minute, Mimosa, I'll open the door."

But Mimosa needed no help. Standing up on her back legs, she pulled the handle down with a front paw and went in.

4 — So, later that day, they drove to the police station.

"A lost cat, eh?" said the sergeant. "I'll have to take some particulars. Now . . . where did I put those forms?"

Mimosa twitched her long thin tail, then twisted it round a drawer-handle. She gave it a little tug, and the drawer slid open.

"Why," gasped the sergeant, "*there's* the very form I was looking for."

Mimosa preened smugly.

"Well," said the surprised officer, "it seems there *was* a lady in here asking about a cat. All in brown, she was. Constable Perkins said she left a long broomstick outside the door. He thought she was one of the cleaners."

"She was a witch," whispered Beccy.

"Oh, yes," said the sergeant, not believing a word of it. "Well, your brown witch left an address for you to contact."

"The Oaks, Hollow-Down Woods," Mrs Dean read out.

3 — "She's a *magic* cat — witches' cats always are," said Beccy.

Mrs Dean only chuckled, then got on with her housework. Beccy and Mimosa looked at each other.

"You *can* work magic, can't you?" whispered Beccy.

Mimosa gave a twitch of her whiskers, then flicked her tail under Beccy's bed and brought out a brooch.

"Goodness! I was looking for that this morning," gasped Beccy. "You *are* magic!"

At bedtime, Mimosa didn't want to leave and so spent the night on a cosy cushion.

"Would you like to come to school with me, Mimosa?" asked Beccy next morning. "You could tell me if words like 'success' have one or two 'c's."

Mimosa twitched her long tail and outlined a large "2".

"Two? Thank you, my pet," said Beccy.

"She's not *your* pet," Beccy's mum reminded her. "We'll call into the police station after school tonight and find out if anyone has reported her missing."

6 — She was going to say more, but Mimosa had dashed across the path and was already twisting her tail round the broomstick the old lady was holding.

Mimosa waved one of her paws and then, with a *whoosh*, they were off. In no time at all, they were a tiny speck in the sky.

"She's gone," sighed Beccy, sadly. "She's gone with the brown witch."

"She's left you a souvenir," her mother pointed out. "There's her collar hanging on one of the branches."

Inside was the tiny piece of paper. "Miss Mimosa Brown" was written on it in scratchy writing.

"I shall leave it behind my bedroom door," said Beccy, "just in case she ever comes back."

"In the meantime," said Mrs Dean, who thought she must have been dreaming, "we'll buy an old-fashioned *tabby* cat, who won't want to go any further than the garden!"

And that's just what they did!

5 — They drove along a country road until they came to Hollow-Down Woods.

"Here we are," said Mrs Dean. "Now we must find a house called The Oaks."

Mimosa gave a loud "caw"!

A high, cracked voice replied, making Beccy and her mother jump.

"So *there* you are, my pretty puss," it said. "I've warned you about preening your whiskers in mid-air. One of these days you'll hurt yourself when you fall off."

Sitting on the stump of an old oak tree was a little old lady in a long brown dress, brown button-up boots and a brown hat.

"The Oaks wasn't a house at all," said Beccy softly. "It was a *tree*."

Now we're off to get our copy of
Twinkle
The picture paper specially for little girls
EVERYBODY IS READING IT!
COME ON!
1992
Little Star
Specially for little girls and little boys
With 16 super activity pages — lots of puzzles, games and things to do!
CAROLS
MRS BUNNY
LOOK OUT TOO FOR THIS SUPER BOOK
NOW ON SALE
SPECIALLY FOR LITTLE GIRLS & BOYS
Price £3.45
EVERY WEEK YOU'LL FIND LOTS OF STORIES, PUZZLES AND THINGS TO DO
Twinkle
ON SALE EVERY WEDNESDAY

NANCY is keen on NURSING.
I'm sure you all know that!
She's very proud of that red cross
She wears upon her hat.

OLIVIA has a pair of OARS,
Inside her rowing boat.
Along the silver stream she sk
And always keeps afloat.

UNA swims UNDERWATER.
Down to the deep she'll go.
But once, a big crab caught her,
And nipped her little toe.

TWINKLE loves story TELLI
Her picture paper's great.
Down at the shop it's selling –
So hurry, don't be late!

VAL has a flair for VAULTING.
Just watch her in the gym . . .
Whoops! Up and over, see her go,
And land so neat and trim.

X is a little mystery girl!
I think she must be *you*.
I wonder what can be your nam
And what you like to do?

WENDY'S a one for WALKING,
In shoes of shiny leather,
And with her pack upon her back,
She never minds the weather.